Chebogue Point

# The Story of the Samson

Kathleen Benner Duble

Illustrated by Alexander Farquharson

iㅇi Charlesbridge

*For Chrissy and Cat Rossi, whose history and experiences are so wonderfully interwoven with those of my daughters. I love you both as if you were my own!*
—K. B. D.

*To my wife, Donna, and my daughter, Rachel—the other artists in my life.*
—A. F.

Text copyright © 2008 by Kathleen Benner Duble
Illustrations copyright © 2008 by Alexander Farquharson

Published by Charlesbridge
85 Main Street
Watertown, MA 02472
(617) 926-0329
www.charlesbridge.com

**Library of Congress Cataloging-in-Publication Data**
Duble, Kathleen Benner.
    The Story of the *Samson* / Kathleen Benner Duble ; illustrated by Alexander Farquharson.
        p. cm.
    ISBN 978-1-58089-183-7 (reinforced for library use)
    ISBN 978-1-58089-184-4 (softcover)
1. *Samson* (Schooner)—History—Juvenile literature.  I. Farquharson, Alexander. II. Title.
G540.D694 2008
910.4'5—dc22                          2007026199

Printed in China
(hc) 10 9 8 7 6 5 4 3 2 1
(sc) 10 9 8 7 6 5 4 3 2 1

Illustrations done in oils on Bristol Board
Display type and text type set in Mayflower and Goudy
Color separations by Chroma Graphics, Singapore
Printed and bound by Regent Publishing Services
Production supervision by Brian G. Walker
Designed by Diane M. Earley

"You want to hear the story again, eh, Sam?" Grandpa asked. "The story of this house?"

Sam nodded and climbed onto his grandpa's bed. He knew every line on his grandpa's face, worn and weathered as it was by the sea. He knew the look of his grandpa's eyes, watery and distant as the ocean's horizon. He knew the sound of his grandpa's voice, which rose and fell like sea waves hitting the shore.

And Sam loved everything about his grandpa's house: how it stood on a bluff above the sea, how it moaned with the wind on stormy nights, how it cracked with delight when the summer Canadian air warmed its wooden boards. But he loved its story most of all.

"I built this house myself," Grandpa said. His voice shook like the air when it quivers with a coming storm. "It's to be yours one day."

Sam knew. His grandfather had told him this before.

"Come then," Grandpa said. "Hand me the book, and I'll tell you about this house of mine, its story and its secrets."

Like a barnacle clings to a rock, Sam snuggled close to his grandpa.

"Well, now," Grandpa began, putting an arm around his grandson, "this story starts with a ship, doesn't it?"

Sam opened the scrapbook to reveal a charcoal sketch of his grandfather with some sailors. "Her name was the *Samson* . . ." Sam added.

"Yes," Grandpa said. "Her name was the *Samson*. And you were named for her."

"Do you think they saw us?" the bridge hand whispered.

"They catch us, it's jail for us all," the first officer muttered.

"The Samson can outrun any customs ship from this distance," I said.

"Still, with our cargo, it's best we're careful," the first officer warned.

"Quiet! Stop your jabbering," the captain hissed.

The large ship loomed on the horizon. We could just make out its shape in the blackness. A sudden light flared into the sky, followed by another and then another.

"Could be distress signals, sir," the bridge hand said.

"Should I alter our course to go help?" I asked the captain.

"No," he ordered. "Don't turn back. That customs ship is just trying to lure us toward them and catch us with these sealskins."

"But what if they're really in trouble?" the first officer asked.

"They aren't," the captain said. "They've tried tricks like this before. Don't turn, I say. Stay on our present course for home. Keep your voices low. Those are my orders."

"And so you went home," Sam said sadly.

"So we went home," Grandpa agreed. "April 14, 1912."

"And it wasn't a customs ship, was it, Grandpa?" Sam said. "It wasn't them trying to catch you illegally sealing, was it? It was the *Titanic*, wasn't it?"

Grandpa's eyes teared up. "Yes, it was the night the *Titanic* hit that iceberg. We didn't reply to their signal, assuming it was a trick. So many people died that night. But I learned something then—don't ever turn away from someone who needs you. You do, and you'll regret it."

Sam nodded. Grandpa said this every time. Sam hated how this part of the story upset his grandpa so.

"But the *Samson* saved people, too," Sam said, quickly turning the page. "Some very famous people."

Grandpa wiped his eyes. "You're right, Sam. She did."

They looked at a magazine article that read, "RESCUED!" next to a photo of some men on an ice pack. The date below the photo— May 21, 1916— was barely visible.

RESCUED! May 21, 1916

The explorers wearily trudged up the snow-covered hill. They had been at sea for fourteen days in the smallest of boats, covering over eight hundred miles. They had survived hurricanes and ice and enormous waves. At last they had reached South Georgia, only to find that they were still seventeen mountainous miles from civilization.

Three men stayed behind, too sick to make the climb. Now the other three walked and slid over glaciers and snowfields, moving steadily forward in spite of the cold and the ice and the winds.

14

They crested a hill and stopped.

"We've made it," one of them whispered, his lips cracked from the cold, his fingers frostbitten from the ice.

Below them lay a small whaling station. They could see a ship just entering the bay.

With tears in their eyes, they hurried on toward food and shelter and the incoming ship with the knowledge that at last, they were saved!

"It was the *Samson* they saw coming into the harbor, Grandpa!" Sam cried out. "She was waiting for them when they reached the base. The *Samson* took them around the island to rescue the men who had been too sick to travel."

"And who was the explorer?" Grandpa asked.

"Ernest Shackleton," Sam answered. "He was an amazing explorer, wasn't he, Grandpa?"

Grandpa nodded his head. "The story of Ernest Shackleton and his men is one of the greatest survival stories ever, and the *Samson* was a small part of it. I was proud of her for having braved those Antarctic waters. And I longed to be back on her decks."

"And so you went," Sam continued. "You signed up to sail with her once more."

"I did," Grandpa said. "And I was there when she made a far more dangerous rescue."

Grandpa turned the page.

There was a photo of Sam's grandpa surrounded by snow and ice and penguins. Sam loved this picture. He laughed, and his grandpa laughed, too.

"This was taken in 1927," Grandpa said. "I was thirty years old. That year Admiral Richard E. Byrd bought the *Samson* and renamed her the *City of New York*."

"Admiral Byrd. Another famous explorer, right, Grandpa?" Sam asked.

"One and the same," Grandpa said.

"He knew the *Samson* was tough enough for Antarctica," said Sam.

"Yep," Grandpa said proudly. "He wanted to take her to explore the polar region, and take her he did."

"Along with you," Sam added.

Grandpa smiled. "Yes, along with me."

"Another storm's brewing, Captain." I motioned toward the darkening sky.

Captain Neville shook his head. "Two storms in seven days. Let's hope this one isn't as bad as the last. We've got to get to Admiral Byrd and the others soon."

I nodded my head in agreement, remembering the gale we had faced only a few days before. The wind had blown us sideways onto the ice, trapping us. It had taken hours to free ourselves. I thought about Admiral Byrd and the other men we had left at the Antarctic base, Little America. We should have arrived to evacuate them weeks ago.

In an hour the storm was on us, blowing icy-cold winds. Most of the men huddled in the hold, tightening blankets against the Antarctic air. They ventured outside only when necessary. The ship tossed and turned and hit hard against the ice floes. Men turned pale and were sick from the rocking and the rolling and the bumping. For days the storm blew and blew. Then suddenly, all was quiet.

The men came out onto the deck. We shielded our eyes, for the sun was brilliant against the white around us. When we looked up at the lines on the masts, we were distraught, for they were covered in thick, heavy ice. Still our hearts were light, for we had survived another storm on that frozen sea.

"Our position, sir?" Captain Neville barked to me. We were both worn from the battle of steering the ship.

I gave him the longitude and latitude.

"Repeat that, please," the captain asked. His face had gone pale.

I gave the numbers again.

The men knew something was wrong, but they didn't know what. I did, of course. I was the navigator. That storm had blown us three hundred miles off course.

"But you did reach the men at the base, right, Grandpa?" Sam asked.

"We did," Grandpa said. "Just in time, we saved Admiral Byrd and the others who were with him. They hadn't much food left nor candles, and the light was fading as winter approached."

Sam thought of the dangers he, too, might face when he was older. He hoped he'd be brave like his grandpa and Admiral Byrd.

"You didn't hear about the ship for a long time after that, did you, Grandpa?" Sam continued, wanting to hear the rest of the story.

"No," Grandpa agreed. "I had moved to Yarmouth, Nova Scotia, to take up fishing. I married your grandma and settled down."

1933 CHICAGO WORLD'S FAIR

BYRD'S SOUTH POLE SHIP

"Then you saw the postcard," Sam interrupted.

Grandpa turned another page, and Sam saw a postcard from the 1933 Chicago World's Fair. Its edges were crinkled with wear.

"I came across this postcard for an exhibition on polar exploration. The exhibit had been housed in a ship, and the ship was . . ."

"The *Samson*!" Sam crowed.

Grandpa laughed. "Yes, the *Samson* had been turned into a museum."

"Step right up. Step right up. Come see artifacts from the only land on earth still shrouded in mystery," called out a man in a straw-brimmed hat. "Don't miss the opportunity to see the sights of the polar region to our south. Step right up."

The man tapped the poster beside him with his cane. "Come on in, folks! Don't miss the little ship that drew enormous crowds to the World's Fair. Last day to see the exhibit that enchanted thousands in Chicago. Tonight we'll be leaving on our tour of the Great Lakes. Wait, and you'll have missed your chance. I guarantee ya she's worth your nickel."

As the Samson gently rode at its mooring in Cleveland that day, people went inside to see the photos, exploration tools, handwritten notes, and stuffed Antarctic animals that had fascinated the crowds at the 1933 World's Fair. They oohed and aahed over everything.

But the next day, as the Samson prepared to leave Cleveland, disaster struck!

25

The Samson's sails were hoisted, flapping noisily in the breeze. The day was clear with a good wind. The ship floated from the dock, sailing proudly away.

"Watch out!" someone yelled into the quiet of the afternoon.

The navigator at her helm looked ahead. "Lower the sails!" he called. The sails were quickly taken down. The Samson drifted a few hundred feet more and then came to an abrupt halt.

The top of her mast was up against the bottom of a newly constructed bridge that had been built while the ship sat at its berth in Cleveland.

The Samson was stuck!

"And you know what happened then, right, Sam?" Grandpa asked.

"They dismantled the *Samson*, and she went to the Caribbean islands!" Sam shouted gleefully.

"Before that," Grandpa said, giving him a warning look.

Sam made a face. "The *Samson* stayed in Cleveland and became a permanent museum for a while. Museums are boring, Grandpa."

"Stop feeding your mind, boy, and it grows useless and feeble," Grandpa gently scolded. "You don't want that, do you?"

Sam shook his head. No, he didn't want that, but the rest of the story was more exciting.

"The *Samson* made many people aware of polar exploration," Grandpa said proudly.

"But then she went to the Caribbean, right, Grandpa?" Sam asked.

Grandpa tousled Sam's hair. "That's right, Sam. During World War II, the *Samson* went to the Caribbean." He turned the page to a letter, dated March 12, 1945, and read it aloud.

March 12, 1945

Dear Sir:

As you may have heard from my folks, I've been stationed in the West Indies and am in charge of arranging the shipment of supplies to our boys at the front.

Two days ago I went down to the harbor and heard one of my servicemen arguing with a sea captain. I turned to see what the source of the argument was and caught my breath. The ship you had told me about over the years, the Samson, was tied up to our dock.

I asked what the problem was, and my serviceman told me that the Samson was blocking our warships.

"See here," the captain argued, "I got a cargo to off-load and some molasses to pick up. Then I'm headed back to Nova Scotia. I won't be long."

I gazed at the Samson. She was majestic against that bright blue sky, yet I could see she was in bad need of repair. I wished I could board her, fix her up, see her sail off once again on her daring adventures.

But there's a war on, and boys are dying. I had to let her go. I ordered the captain to move her around the island. He marched angrily toward the Samson, and I watched the ship leave her berth. I'm sorry to say this, sir, but her future looks grim. This may be the last time any of us sees the Samson sail.

Sincerely,
S.Sgt. Tommy Wallace

31

"Tommy never made it back, did he, Grandpa?" asked Sam.

"No," Grandpa whispered, "he didn't. He was sent to the Pacific and was killed in action. Tommy used to live next door. I had seen him grow into a fine young man. A lot of good lives were lost in that war." Grandpa sighed.

"But the *Samson*," Sam said, pulling his grandpa's thoughts away from that sadness, "she lives still . . ."

"Whoa, whoa," Grandpa said, holding up his hand and laughing. "You're rushing the story, Sam. You must never hurry an old person's story."

Sam smiled. Grandpa told him this all the time. And he had learned to wait patiently for his grandpa's stories most of the time, but not with this one. For he loved this story best of all.

"The *Samson* was old . . ." Grandpa continued.

". . . but she was not finished," Sam added.

"Right," Grandpa agreed. "In spite of her age, she sailed on, carrying cargo, carrying coal."

"But then she broke her propeller shaft," Sam said, turning the page to a newspaper clipping, yellowed and wrinkled with time. "She had to be towed up north to be repaired, and you read about it in the paper."

"Yes. I went and stood on the shore in Yarmouth that day in 1952. I watched her leave the harbor for Lunenberg."

"But she never made it," Sam said, shaking his head.

"No," Grandpa said, "she didn't."

From the shoreline I could see a towboat pulling the Samson out to sea. Her sails were lowered, her decks were covered in a layer of coal dust, and her hull was peppered with barnacles. She was old and tired.

Suddenly everyone on the towboat began shouting and waving. The Samson had broken her towline and was headed toward land, pulled on a tide that was fast and strong.

Six men were on the Samson, racing around trying to save her. They weren't quick enough.

The Samson hit land with a crash that could be heard a great distance away. Flames leapt from her deck.

In horror I watched the men on board leap into the cold Canadian waters. I kept watch until I saw them safely pulled on board the towboat.

Then I turned back to the Samson. Bright with flames she quickly filled with water and sank into the shallow waters off Chebogue Ledge until only her masts were visible. I felt as if I was sinking with her: my life, my past, everything I was, descended into the dark of that sea.

"Grandpa," Sam said, "you always get so sad at this part."

"Well, it was a sad time, Sam," Grandpa said gruffly.

"Just for a while," Sam protested.

"It was a tragedy," Grandpa said sternly.

"There are ways to recover from all tragedies, Grandpa," said Sam.

"Really?" Grandpa asked. "Who told you that?"

"You did!" Sam said.

"So tell me then," the old man said, smiling, "how did the
*Samson* do it?"

Sam grinned.  He loved it when Grandpa let him tell this part
of the story.

Storms hit the coast off Nova Scotia hard that night. Rain pelted windows. Wind howled. No one was about. Nothing moved. The land had an eerie emptiness to it.

But the sea, she was wild, thrashing and moaning with the wind and the rain. Below the waters, the tides churned, pushing and pulling on all the creatures they harbored, pushing and pulling on the Samson.

Slowly, the Samson yielded. First one, then another of her boards separated. They went with the tides and the winds, floating upward, floating inward. When dawn came, the Samson lay in pieces on the beach, littering the shore.

Grandpa wiped at his eyes, pretending to dry tears.

"Grandpa," Sam said, laughing, "stop it. You rescued the *Samson* from the beach, remember? She still lives!"

"How is that possible?" Grandpa asked, smiling.

"Because you built this whole house with her!" Sam cried out triumphantly.

"And so I did, Sam. So I did. And there you have your story," Grandpa said as he closed the book.

Sam sighed. He looked around at the house. He could hear the sound of waves in its floorboards and smell the salt in its walls. He had grown up safely harbored in a ship. Like his grandpa, he had sailed upon the *Samson*.

Sam turned back to his grandpa to make him tell the story again, but Grandpa had fallen asleep. Sam watched his grandpa's chest rise slowly up and down, like a ship rides the tide.

Softly, Sam climbed down from the bed and went outside, taking the book with him. He sat down on the porch, on the *Samson's* decks. The wind tossed his hair. In the distance he saw freighters leaving to cross the sea. He heard waves crashing against the rocks below. Sam shivered with delight, determined to cross those seas and brave those waves himself someday.

And there, with the ship's wood warming him in the late afternoon sun, Sam opened the book and once again read *The Story of the* Samson to himself—right from the beginning.

# Timeline for the *Samson*

**1885**

K. Larsen builds the *Samson* in Arendal, Norway. For twenty-seven years the crew harvests seals in the frigid waters of the Greenland Sea and the Arctic Ocean.

**April 14, 1912**

After an unsuccessful sealing season north of Iceland, the *Samson* sails to the Grand Banks, shoals in the West Atlantic Ocean, looking for better sealing grounds. There the crew allegedly sees and ignores flares from the *Titanic* right before she sinks.

**May 21, 1916**

Having been refitted as a whaler when the seal supply dwindled, the *Samson* enters the harbor at South Georgia, headed for Stromness Whaling Station. There she is spotted by Ernest Shackleton and his crew as they finally reach safety after having endured ocean waves, hurricanes, and bitter cold.

**1927**

The *Samson* is bought by Admiral Richard E. Byrd on the advice of Roald Amundsen, another polar explorer who had once sailed on the *Samson*. She is rerigged for her new job as an exploration ship and renamed the *City of New York*.

**January 1930**

The *Samson* proves her worthiness, fighting heavy storms and seas to reach Admiral Byrd and his men at Little America, Antarctica.

## Summer 1933

The Chicago World's Fair opens, and the *Samson* makes an appearance, displaying artifacts from Antarctica.

## 1934-1944

Following the World's Fair, the *Samson* tours the Great Lakes as a museum of polar exploration. Her home base is Cleveland, Ohio.

## 1944-1952

The *Samson* is bought by Captain Lou Kenedy for $1,000 and refitted to become a cargo vessel. She carries coal and molasses between the Caribbean and Nova Scotia. Her route is constant, even during World War II.

## December 29, 1952

The *Samson* sinks off Chebogue Ledge in Canada.

## January 5, 1953

All hope of salvaging the *Samson* is abandoned. Her remnants are used by locals to build houses.

## Summer 1977

*The Story of the* Samson is set in Canada in the late 1970s. Sam and Grandpa are fictional characters. The *Samson* and her adventures, however, are true. (See Author's Note, page 44.)

# Author's Note

My parents first heard the story of the *Samson* on a trip to Nova Scotia. Their guide told them of a ship that had possibly been present when the *Titanic* sank and had also been used by Admiral Richard E. Byrd during his Antarctic explorations. The guide claimed that his grandfather had built his house from the wreckage of the ship after she washed ashore on the coast of Nova Scotia. My parents mentioned all this casually to me, but the story struck a chord. I began to research.

The *Samson* was built in Norway in 1885. As a sealing schooner, she needed to withstand ice and cold seas. She measured 147.9 feet long, 21.1 feet wide, had 2 decks, and carried a crew of 45. She sailed for 67 years, first as a sealing schooner, then as a whaler, an exploration ship, a museum, and finally a trade ship. She was part of an incredible amount of history, including the rescue of Ernest Shackleton's crewmates, explorations to Antarctica with Admiral Byrd, and an appearance at the 1933 Chicago World's Fair.

Her biggest claim to fame was allegedly being the mystery boat seen by survivors of the *Titanic*. In 1962, on the 50th anniversary of the sinking of the *Titanic*, first officer Henrik Naess came forward on a BBC radio program. He was on the *Samson* in 1912 and claimed to have seen the *Titanic's* distress signals. He told listeners that the *Samson* had not responded to the flares because she was violating territorial waters.

However, his testimony is disputed. In his book *The Ship That Stood Still*, Leslie Reade places the *Samson* far from the area where the *Titanic* went down, using photocopied government tax documents as proof. The truth may never be known for certain.

The remnants of the *Samson* rest now in Nova Scotia. Some of its wood was used to build various houses. Other relics can be found in the Yarmouth Museum. The ship may be gone, but her story still lives and breathes. For me, the *Samson* represents the miracle of life, with all its twists and turns. Life leads each of us to experiences yet to be imagined, making us all a part of history.

# Resources

## Books

Eaton, John P., and Charles A. Haas. Titanic: *Triumph and Tragedy*. 2nd ed. New York: Norton, 1995.

Gardiner, Robin, and Dan Van der Vat. *The* Titanic *Conspiracy: Cover-ups and Mysteries of the World's Most Famous Sea Disaster*. New York: Carol Publishing Group, 1996.

Sweeney, E. M. Samson, *The* Titanic's *Mystery Ship*. Nova Scotia, Canada: The Yarmouth Connection, Yarmouth County Historical Society, 1999.

## Websites (Please note that some sites incorrectly refer to the *Samson* as the *Sampson*.)

The Great Ocean Liners: *Californian*, 1902–1915
**http://www.greatoceanliners.net/californian.html**
> An informative look at the *Californian*, whose crew claimed to see a mystery ship in the ice field near the *Titanic*. Also offers a detailed account of the events surrounding the *Titanic* disaster.

Haze Gray Photo Feature: *City of New York*—Admiral Byrd's Exploration Ship
**http://www.hazegray.org/features/cityofny**
> Archive photos and simple text tell the story of the *Samson's* travels after she was purchased by Admiral Byrd and renamed the *City of New York*.

The *Samson's* Strange Sights
**http://home.earthlink.net/~dnitzer/50therships/Samson.html**
> This site details the controversy between Henrik Naess's statement and Leslie Reade's research on the *Samson*.

Web*Titanic*—Other Liners—*Californian*
**http://www.webtitanic.net/framecal.html**
> This site offers an account of what happened on board the *Californian* after the *Titanic* hit an iceberg, and discusses the *Samson*.

The *City of New York* (a.k.a. *Samson*), circa 1930, returns to New York having completed Admiral Richard E. Byrd's first Antarctic expedition. Reproduced by permission from AP Images.